JOVINDA AND NOLI

A WOLVES OF VIMAR PREQUEL

V. M. SANG

To my friends and family who have put up with me writing, and not paying proper attention to them.

A CLASH OF CULTURES

A SPECIAL MESSENGER DELIVERED THE LETTER. JOVINDA'S father took it into his study to open it, but Jovinda saw the Royal seal pressed into the wax. She longed to rush in to her father and ask him why the King was sending him messages. Her eyes kept straying to the door, hoping he would soon come and let them all know what the message said. But she had to wait until after the evening meal before he revealed what the letter contained.

As soon as they finished eating, her father took both Jovinda and her mother into his study. Looking at his daughter he waved the letter. "Is this why you've been so restless, Jo?" He grinned, lifted his glasses onto his nose and read it to them.

King Frome I has the pleasure of inviting Guildmaster Kendo, his wife, Ellire, and daughter, Jovinda, to a reception and ball at the Palace to welcome the Trade Delegation from Rindissillaron to Grosmer.

On Kassidar 10 at the 14th hour of the day.

Jovinda's eyes opened wide and she clapped her hands. "I'm invited to the banquet as well?" She could hardly believe it.

"You're sixteen now, Jo," Ellire said. "It's time you went to be presented at court."

Her father smiled at her excitement, running his hands through his auburn hair, so like Jovinda's own. "All the leaders of the guilds and their families will be there. As part of my family, and a young lady now of age, you are included."

Although not of the nobility, as the supreme leader of all the guilds in Bluehaven, Kendo would be involved in any trade treaties that might be signed between Grosmer and Rindissil-laron, the elven homeland. This banquet was of great importance.

Ellire smoothed the skirts of her dress as she stood. "This is a big occasion, Jo. Tomorrow we'll go to the dressmaker and choose some fabric and a style for your dress."

Jovinda could hardly keep still. To go to the Royal Palace in Aspirilla. To meet the King and his family. Her eyes shone and she turned to her mother as she spoke.

"What colour do you think I should wear? What kind of fabric? Should I have an elaborate dress or a simple style? What will the other girls being presented wear?"

Ellire laughed at her daughter's excitement. "Kassidar is spring, but it can still be cold. We'll need to be aware of that in choosing something. A dress with short sleeves in case it's warm, but with a jacket or shawl you can put on if it turns cool later in the evening. The banquet is only five sixdays away. There will be a lot of people wanting clothes." She paused and wrinkled her brow. "We'll go to Madame Frimb."

Jovinda pressed her hand against her mouth. "Madame Frimb? But she's the most expensive dressmaker in Bluehaven."

Kendo put his arm round her. "Nothing but the very best will be good enough for my daughter's first banquet and ball."

Jovinda rushed up the stairs, nearly tripping over the skirts of her dress in her excitement. She must go and tell her best friend, Salor that she was going to the Palace.

* * *

Jovinda's parents had booked rooms at the Swan in Flight in Aspirilla, the capital of Grosmer. The city stood on an island, known as Holy Isle, because all the churches of the various gods had their headquarters there. The legendary King Sauvern had chosen this place for his capital. He united the warring kings, creating the land of Grosmer. What had once been separate kingdoms were now the six dukedoms of the country.

The landlord of this expensive inn behaved more like the host of a large country house. He treated his customers as important guests and greeted them all personally.

"Welcome to The Swan in Flight, Guildmaster Kendo. Madam Ellire, we are delighted to have you stay with us. And Miss Jovinda, too. Is this your first time in Asperilla, Miss?"

Jovinda blushed at being singled out. "Y-Yes. I've been looking forward to it."

"And now you are here. You must see as much as you can in the time you have, although I have no doubt you'll come back often."

A man, in the livery of a butler, approached them. "Allow me to show you to your rooms."

He took them up a flight of stairs and along a landing with doors on each side. He unlocked two and showed them into the rooms. Then he bowed and left.

Jovinda had a room next to that of her parents. She stopped inside the door and stared. A four-poster bed stood to the left of the door in the large room. It had green drapes embroidered with flowers and birds. Carved flowers decorated the posts and the tester that covered the top of the bed. Rails ran along the tester so the drapes could be closed to keep out draughts.

She ran into the room and bounced on the bed. It would be comfortable. A knock at the door made her get up and smooth down the green bedspread as she did so. Opening the door, she admitted a porter carrying her trunk.

"Thank you," she said. "Please put the trunk over there," indicating a place next to the bed. She reached for her purse. Her parents had taught her to give a tip to servants in other people's households. She handed over a copper royal. The porter bowed and left the room.

Jovinda looked around the room. A fire burned in the fireplace opposite the bed, and two chairs, upholstered in yellow fabric, stood on either side. At the far side of the bed, a table, covered with a yellow and green cloth, held a wash bowl and jug in green pottery.

A bay window with a window seat overlooked the street. She sat on it and gazed out of the window where she could see other guests arriving. Women wearing elegant dresses that swept the floor, and men in smart breeches and tunics descended from the carriages. The people would not wear their best for travelling, she knew, but they all looked so smart.

She was engrossed in the scene and when she heard a knock on her door she tore herself reluctantly away from the window.

"Come in."

The door opened and a maid entered. She curtseyed to Jovinda, who managed to repress a smile at the thought of someone curtseying to her. Although wealthy, Jovinda's family was not of the nobility. They did not have the array of servants that the very rich could afford. Jovinda did not have her own maid and usually dressed herself.

"Please, Miss, I've come to unpack for you. Would you like

me to put out your dress for this evening, or should I come back later?"

"Oh! Well..." Jovinda's thoughts were all on the coming banquet and ball but she managed to recover her wits. "I'll wear the yellow one tonight. Thank you."

She returned to her post by the window as the maid unpacked her clothes and hung them up in the wardrobe next to the fireplace. Carriages continued to roll up. People climbed out and the drivers unloaded trunks and cases and carried them to the inn. Some of the people Jovinda knew, but many she did not. Families arrived, couples, people on their own, all chattering and greeting friends and acquaintances.

I'm not the only one to be excited. It seems as if everyone is as thrilled as I am to be invited to this banquet and ball. Most of these people will have been here before, though. I wonder why they're behaving as if it's all new? Is it because of the elves?

She saw her best friend Salor and her parents and brother getting out of a carriage pulled by two grey horses. She leaned out of the window and tried to catch Salor's attention. She longed to shout to her friend, but knew her parents would be appalled at such common behaviour, so she contented herself with a wave.

Salor saw her and waved back, mouthing "See you later."

When the train of carriages died to a mere trickle Jovinda turned away from the window. There came a rat-a-tat on her door and it opened to admit her mother.

"Aren't you getting dressed yet?" She picked up the yellow dress lying on the bed. "You decided on this one for this evening, then? I hope you've made sure the one for the banquet is hung up. It would never do to have it creased. Not after all the money it cost."

Jovinda bounded across the room, grinning. "I was watching the arrivals. There are lots of important people coming here.

Will there be enough rooms for them all? I suppose there must, or they'd not come here, would they?"

"Well, dear, it is a large inn, but some people will have just come to eat and be staying elsewhere. Some in the Palace itself, I expect. Now get dressed and I'll come and brush your hair."

The maid came in with a jug of hot water that she poured into the wash bowl on the table.

"Do you want me to help you dress, Miss?"

Jovinda shook her head. "No, thank you, I can manage." *After all, I don't have a maid at home. I'm used to dressing myself.*

Ellire came back as promised and brushed Jovinda's auburn hair until it shone. Her hair had a slight curl and hung to her shoulders.

"We should put your hair up tomorrow for the ball," Ellire said. "It would look so much more elegant than hanging loose."

Jovinda shook her head. "I think it looks better as it is now, especially with my dress for tomorrow."

"But, Jo, dear, you want to look your best to meet the royal family. Now, let me help you on with your dress."

Jovinda decided to leave the hair argument until the next day. With her mother fussing over everything, she climbed into the yellow dress that swept the floor, clinging to her slim figure.

Her mother helped her do up the buttons that ran up the back. Jovinda looked at herself in the long mirror standing behind the door. She saw a girl with auburn hair loosely curling around her shoulders. The bodice of the pale yellow dress fitted her curves and the sweetheart neckline showed a hint of décolletage. The skirt clung to her hips and then swept down to the ground, spreading out as it did so. A frill spiralled around it from her waist to the hem.

"Now put these earrings in and this necklace." Ellire stood

back. "You look lovely, darling. Those frills on the skirt of your dress give it that bit extra something."

Jovinda looked down at the said frills. *I wasn't sure about them before, but Mother was right—again. They do add something.*

She looked at her mother, dressed in a powder blue dress. The dress had a pleated skirt and a bodice covered sequins so that whenever she moved, lights glinted all over. It had long sleeves and fastened up to the neck.

"I like your dress, Mother. That colour suits you."

Ellire 's hair looked immaculate, piled up on top of her head. Jovinda frowned slightly as she noticed a few strands of grey. *I've not noticed them before. But I suppose they show up more with her hair being so dark. Father might have them but they won't show as much in hair like mine.*

The family descended the stairs and the butler showed them into a drawing room. People thronged the room, some sitting and some standing, all dressed in fine clothes.

She hesitated at the door, not having been used to so many people all together. I can hardly believe the noise of talking. No one is shouting, but it's almost deafening.

Her father ushered them into the room, then, spotting a colleague from his own guild of Merchants, he apologised and went over to talk. Her mother also saw an old friend and led her daughter in her direction.

Jovinda noticed Salor across the room. Her friend waved. "Mother, there's Salor. I'm going to talk to her."

She rushed over to her friend. Her hazel eyes met Salor's blue ones. "Salor, there are so many people here. Look at this fine room." She swept her hand around encompassing everything. "I never thought an inn would have such wonderful rooms as this. My bedroom is magnificent."

"This is the Swan in Flight. Jo. It's renowned all over Grosmer as being the best. Of course it has magnificent facilities."

"Oh, Salor, my stomach turns over when I think about tomorrow. I'm going to meet the King and Queen! Me, Jovinda. An ordinary girl from Bluehaven. There'll be lots of important people there, too. Will I make an idiot of myself? How will I know what to do?"

Salor looked at her friend with her head on one side. "I know what you're thinking. I was as nervous as you last year, but I assure you it'll be all right. Someone will tell you where to go and when, and the King and Queen are friendly. Anyway, You'll have your name called, shake hands, curtsey and that'll be that. And you're not 'an ordinary girl.' Your father is an important man in the guilds, that makes you not ordinary at all. What's more, he's wealthy."

Jovinda sighed and looked at her hands. "I hope you're right. It would be so-o embarrassing to make a mistake. Suppose I trip on my dress as I'm going up to see the King and Queen?"

At that moment, the landlord came into the drawing room. "Dinner is served, Ladies and Gentlemen." He led the guests to the dining room.

Round tables were scattered around the room. Jovinda's parents managed to get one with Salor's parents, which pleased the girls.

The meal commenced with an entree consisting of a pancake stuffed with tomatoes, mushrooms and herbs. This was followed by roast goose. A variety of local cheeses followed and the meal finished with a light dessert of fruit. The best wines of the region were served throughout the meal, but Ellire kept a close eye on how much Jovinda drank. She frowned at the girl when she thought her daughter had drunk enough.

After the meal, a harpist and a singer entertained the guests in the drawing room. Salor and Jovinda sat in a corner near a window.

"Do you think Prince Gerim will be at the banquet?" Jovinda asked Salor as they sat drinking small cups of coffee.

"He might be, I suppose. Why are you asking? There'll be elves there, Jovinda. Elves! I've never seen an elf. The elves weren't here last year. Do you think they might seat me near one?"

"Why are you interested in elves?"

"And why are you interested in the Prince? He's younger than you, after all."

"He'll be king when his father dies and whoever marries him will be queen."

Salor laughed. "He'll be able to have his pick of all the girls in Grosmer. He'll pick a noble girl I expect. I don't think he'll look at the likes of us."

The girls continued to chatter until their parents told them that, of age or not, they should retire for the night.

The next day, Jovinda and her parents walked around Aspirilla. Narrow cobbled streets ran at right angles from the wide main road that led up to the Palace. Jovinda exclaimed at everything. They visited the temples and the Oracle, although did not ask for a reading.

"She always says something in words no one can understand until after the event has passed. Then, everyone says 'Oh, so that's what she meant,'" Ellire said.

The day passed quickly and soon they returned to the inn to get ready for the banquet and ball. Jovinda won the argument over her hair, and when she had put on her dress, Ellire agreed that the girl had been right.

* * *

Jovinda and her parents stood at the top of the stairs leading down to the reception room in the Palace. Jovinda scanned the room looking for Prince Gerim. The prince was not quite sixteen, but would be at such an important banquet as the heir to the throne. She frowned slightly as she noticed a young elf watching her as she descended the stairs.

Ellire had decided the best style for her dress for the banquet would be, not like the elaborate dresses they saw hanging in Madame Frimb's workroom, but a simple style.

Jovinda saw the green velvet fabric and fell in love with the colour. Ellire agreed it would look good on her, and then went to discuss a style with Madame Frimb. The dress she now wore had a high neckline with small pearl buttons sewn around it. The buttons continued down the centre of the otherwise plain bodice with sleeves that stopped at her elbow. They also had pearl buttons around the cuffs. The skirt flared from her waist giving room for her feet to move when dancing, and more pearl buttons graced the hem. She wore small pearl drops in her ears and a white orchid in her hair.

The family walked down the stairs as a butler announced them. Jovinda stared around. The stairs descended from the balcony where they had entered, and flared out towards the bottom. A red carpet ran down the centre. Large floor to ceiling windows to her right opened onto the Palace gardens, and doors carved with vines and fruits stood open on the opposite side. Torches in sconces lit the room, and glinted on the gold-leaf that covered the cornice. More gold covered a few chairs scattered around for those unable to stand for long, and at the opposite end of the room was a dais with two thrones, again, covered in gold leaf.

A waiter brought a tray of drinks. Jovinda took a glass of

Perimo, a sparkling wine from the islands, as she chatted with many of her parents' friends and acquaintances, feeling very grown up.

Suddenly, a horn sounded. Everyone stopped talking and looked towards the stairs. The Royal Family entered and made their way through the crowd to the dais. As they passed, people bowed their heads or curtseyed. Once the King and Queen settled onto their thrones, the butler announced the first of the young people to be presented.

As it was her first social occasion, Jovinda was one of those young people. When the butler called her name, she looked at her father who mouthed "Go on, Jo". Her mother gave her a little push to start her on her way.

She took a deep breath to try to calm her racing heart, and ascended the dais where she curtseyed to the King and Queen.

The King smiled and his eyes twinkled. "We are delighted to meet you, Jovinda. Enjoy the occasion. There's nothing quite like your first ball."

Then she moved on. Prince Gerim smiled at her and shook her hand. "Pleased to meet you, Miss Jovinda."

Jovinda curtseyed. *He's quite good-looking. I wonder if I can attract his attention? He may even ask me to dance. I wonder what kind of girls he likes?*

The call came for everyone to go into the banqueting hall and be seated. Jovinda was surprised to be seated well away from her parents. She found herself sitting between a young man she knew, whose father was the head of the leatherworkers' guild, and a handsome young elf—the very same elf she had seen watching her as she descended the stairs. She drew eyebrows together.

The elf turned to her and asked her name.

"Jovinda. What's yours?"

He laughed. "I doubt you'd be able to pronounce it," His smile lit up his deep blue eyes.

"Try me."

"Well, it's Nolimissalloran, but you can call me Noli. All my friends do."

Jovinda looked at the elf. *He's very handsome.*

His extraordinary eyes fascinated her. They were slanting, like those of all elves, but it was their colour that attracted her attention. They were a deep blue. Much deeper than any eyes she had ever seen before. She no longer felt an interest in capturing the attention of Prince Gerim.

After the banquet, the king announced that the ball would commence in thirty minutes in the ballroom. Everyone left the tables and stood around in groups talking.

When the music began, people started to move toward it. Noli held out his arm to Jovinda, beating the young man who had sat on her other side at the banquet. She took it, blushing, and the pair strolled into the ballroom.

As they passed through the double doors, Jovinda's mouth fell open. She would have stopped in her tracks if Noli had not been urging her forward.

The chandeliers hanging from the ceiling cast dancing lights around the room as the candles flickered in the currents of air. Everywhere she looked she saw gold leaf. On the carving on the dais, on the thrones for the king and queen, on the urns in niches on the walls.

A delicate blue paint covered the walls,on which were painted scenes of dancing couples, The ceiling was painted a deeper blue with stars covering it.

The quartet on the raised dais was playing a jolly tune and people were beginning to drift onto the dance floor.

"May I have this first dance?" Noli bowed to Jovinda. She nodded her assent.

He swept her into his arms and whirled her around the floor. Noli was an excellent dancer and she found herself dancing better than she had ever done before. He was so easy to follow.

After the dance Noli escorted her to a seat at a small table occupied by her parents. They were sitting with Salor and her parents. He bowed and drifted off towards a group of elves.

Jovinda watched him go. He bowed to one of the young female elves and escorted her onto the dance floor.

"Jo." It was her mother speaking. "Jo, Krombo is asking you to dance. What's wrong with you?"

"Oh! Sorry, Krombo." She rose and they joined the dancing couples.

A constant stream of young men came to dance with Jovinda. Some danced well, but some were clumsy. None danced as well as Noli. She kept looking around to see with whom the young elf was dancing.

Does he like her better than he likes me?

This thought ran through her head over and over again whenever Noli danced with another young woman. All thoughts of the Prince fled as she watched the handsome elf.

He asked her to dance again before leaving her once more to dance with others. But he danced with her more than anyone else, and danced the last dance with her.

All too soon the evening ended and Jovinda and her parents took a carriage back to The Swan in Flight. They were leaving the next morning for the ferry back to Bluehaven. Jovinda found herself hoping she would see Noli again. After all, if he stayed with the delegation, then he would be based in Bluehaven. She smiled.

"What are you grinning at?" her father asked her.

"Oh, nothing. Only that I had a really good time this evening."

* * *

The day after the family arrived home in the rich quarter of Bluehaven, a messenger arrived with a bouquet of flowers addressed to "Jovinda, the most beautiful girl at the King's banquet." It was signed Nolimissalloran of House Diplomat.

Jovinda clapped her hands when she realised Noli had remembered her, especially as he called her 'the most beautiful girl at the banquet.'

She told Salor, who laughed. "You've soon forgotten Prince Gerim. What about your ambition to become Queen?"

Jovinda looked at her from the corner of her eyes and smiled. "Oh, I've not forgotten that. Can't I enjoy the flattery of a handsome elf as well?"

It did not end there. Noli came to call on her a few days later. The two went for a walk in a park not far away from Jovinda's home. As they walked, Noli told her tales of his homeland, far across the continent of Khalram.

"Many who are not elves, and who visit Rindissillaron don't think the city is there," he told her.

"I've heard rumours that the elven mages have made the city invisible."

He laughed. "No, that's not true. The houses are built in the treetops, and there are walkways linking them—all high in the trees. Unless you look up, you won't see them."

"That's amazing."

"You'd love it. Our main inn is built in the trunk of a hollow tree. They put on shows by travelling entertainers. And the songs the elves sing at sunrise and sunset are beautiful. They praise Grillon for his guardianship."

"How I wish I could see it. It sounds a wonderful place," Jovinda said with a sigh. "All those trees."

Noli nodded. "I don't like it in human cities very much. There's not enough green, and the air seems thick."

"You'd like to go back to Rindiss...Rindiss... ?"

"Rindissillaron. Yes, I'd like to go back, but we have a job to do here. It mightn't be too bad, though, with a beautiful girl like you to talk to." He grinned.

Jovinda looked at him through her lashes. "Do you really think I'm beautiful."

He stopped and took her arm, pulling her close to him. Her heart beat faster and faster as he turned her to face him. "You are the most beautiful girl I've ever seen."

He stepped away, and Jovinda's heart began to settle down. *The most beautiful girl he's ever seen? Does he mean me? With all the beautiful elves he must have seen?*

They walked in silence for a while, until it was time for Jovinda to return home.

When they arrived at the door of her parents' house they stood looking at one another.

"I have to go in," Jovinda said, looking at the ground.

Noli nodded. "Yes, I suppose you do."

They continued standing there, Noli looking at Jovinda, and Jovinda looking at the ground.

"We should do this again," the elf said.

It was Jovinda's turn to nod. She then looked up into his eyes which had turned to indigo. "Yes, Noli. I'd like that." *Don't seem too keen. You're not a girl from the docks. Don't push yourself onto him.*

But she found it difficult to keep her cool. She could hardly believe such a handsome man as Noli could be interested in her.

When next she saw Salor she talked about him until the

other girl said. "It looks as if you've forgotten about marrying Prince Gerim."

"Oh, that was a silly girl's pipe dream. Noli is much better than any prince could ever be."

"Are you sure it's not his difference that attracts you?"

"Oh, Salor, how can you say such a thing. He's handsome, witty, kind, interesting and oh, everything a girl could wish for." She clapped her hands.

* * *

Jovinda sat in her room. Noli had not visited her for three days. Perhaps he wasn't as interested as he claimed. She did her best to fulfil her tasks, but she kept looking out of the window in the hope of seeing him walking up the road towards the house.

Ellire called to her daughter. "Jo, would you like to come with me to visit your Uncle Saminlow? He's been in bed with heart trouble these last few days. I think he'd like to see you. You know how he always made a fuss of you when you were little."

Jovinda got ready and walked the few streets to her Uncle's house with her mother. But she kept glancing back to see if she could see Noli coming to visit her.

As soon as they got home after the visit, Promin approached her. "A note for you, Miss."

Jovinda's heart jumped. Could this be from Noli? Had she missed seeing him? She ran up to her room and opened the note.

Dear Jovinda,

I was disappointed not to find you in. I'm sorry it's been three whole days since we went for that wonderful walk. I've been kept very busy working since then and have been unable to visit until now. I will call again tomorrow and perhaps we can go for another walk.

Noli

Jovinda read the note again, then for a third time. Cradling it to her breast, she grinned. But what time would he come? He had not said in the note.

The next morning, Jovinda got up feeling light as the puffs of cloud floating across the blue sky. *It's not as blue as Noli's eyes, though.*

She skipped down the stairs humming a song, and entered the dining room for breakfast.

"Good morning, Jo." Her father greeted her with a kiss. "You seem happy this morning."

She grinned at him. "Yes, it's a beautiful morning, Daddy. The sun is shining and spring is truly on the way."

"Get your breakfast from the sideboard, Jo," her mother said. "and come and sit down."

Jovinda collected a boiled egg and some bread and sat at the table. Promin did not serve the family at breakfast.

As a young lady of some standing, Jovinda learned music, art and needlework, as well as reading and writing and simple arithmetic. This morning her music teacher was due.

She sat on the stool and picked up her lute. Try as she might, she could not concentrate and made mistakes where she had previously been perfect. But Noli had said he would visit her today. When would he come? Had he forgotten? Had something come up that he had to see to?

After the disastrous lesson, her music teacher threw up his hands and left muttering about erratic young girls, and Promin called the family to lunch.

Jovinda picked at her food, and afterwards decided to sew to pass the time. She sat opposite her mother in the elaborately furnished room. It was a cool day for spring, in spite of the sunshine, and a fire burned in the grate. Yellow curtains gave a light feel, and chairs upholstered in blue made the room seem summery. Two windows overlooked the street, but when the knock came at the door, Jovinda jumped up and almost ran from the room.

"Jo!" her mother called her back. "We have a butler to answer the door."

Almost immediately, Promin showed Noli into the room.

"Good afternoon, Madame Ellire. Good afternoon, Miss Jovinda." Noli bowed.

"Good afternoon," replied Ellire, holding out her hand.

Noli bowed and kissed the proffered hand. Jovinda smothered a giggle that the elf had kissed her mother's hand instead of shaking it. She looked at her Ellire, wondering if she felt confused, too. Noli was certainly gallant.

"Do sit down." Ellire indicated a chair. "To what do we owe the pleasure of this visit?"

Noli sank into the indicated chair. "I was hoping I could take a walk with Miss Jovinda. She and I have become friends since meeting at the King's banquet." His eyes strayed to where Jovinda sat, her sewing lying idle in her lap.

"Yes, of course I'll come for a walk with you, Noli." Her heart began to beat faster and someone was stirring her stomach with a large spoon. Would her mother object to her going for a walk with Noli? No, she couldn't. She was sixteen now and an adult. But habits die hard and, adult or not, Jovinda felt anxious.

"Don't be late back or dinner will be cold," Ellire called as they left the room.

Jovinda caught a glimpse of her mother's frown as she said this, but brushed it to one side in her joy at being with Noli.

* * *

Over the next few months, Noli became a regular caller on Jovinda. Her stomach churned whenever he knocked on the door. They walked all over Bluehaven and into the countryside around. Some days, Noli managed to borrow a pony and trap from the Embassy and on those days they went farther.

One day, deep into summer, when Noli was driving the trap in the woods outside Bluehaven, it hit a bump in the road. Jovinda lost her balance. Noli immediately reached out and, putting his arm around her, prevented her from falling. She instinctively leaned into him. He halted the pony and pulled Jovinda towards him. She was sure he could hear her heart beating as he bent his head and kissed her gently on the lips.

"I thought you were going to fall."

Jovinda could say nothing. She felt the colour rise into her cheeks as she stared into his blue eyes.

"Are you angry with me? Perhaps I shouldn't have kissed you."

She shook her head. Nothing existed for her except those amazing eyes.

"Jo, I've never felt like I feel when I'm with you. My heart races when I hear your name. All the butterflies in the world have taken residence in my stomach and fly around when I see you. I hope and pray that you feel something for me."

Jovinda did not know what to say. She knew that whenever she saw Noli, her heart started racing. She knew when he spoke it was the sweetest sound in the world, and she knew when his hand brushed hers, those butterflies Noli spoke of all flew to her stomach.

"Noli," she eventually managed to say, "I didn't know anyone could feel like this. It's wonderful. You are wonderful."

He pulled her closer. The butterflies once more took off. Cupping her chin in his hand, he brushed his lips on hers. She thought she would explode. As he drew away she forgot all the teaching of her mother about how a well brought up girl should behave, and she pulled his head back. This time the kiss was long and deep.

When it finished, she sighed and rested her head on his shoulder as he trotted the trap back to town. She had never felt so happy.

"Jo, I love you more than I can say. I will love you forever, no matter what happens. Remember that I will love you young or old, well or sick. I will never leave you. I couldn't live if I did."

"And I love you, too, Noli."

This is the best thing that has ever happened to me. And he loves me, too.

* * *

But that was not what her parents thought.

Ellire called Jovinda into the drawing room. "Jo, dear, please sit down. I must talk to you."

Ellire looked so serious Jovinda thought someone must be sick or even have died. Was it her Uncle Saminlow? He had seemed a little better when she visited him with her mother.

"What is it, Mother?" She sat in a comfortable chair opposite Ellire.

"We must talk about that young man, Noli, dear."

Jovinda frowned and looked at her hands. What was her mother going to say? They liked Noli, she knew, and while they had not exactly encouraged their friendship, they had not prevented the pair from seeing each other. She waited to see what was coming next.

"While the pair of you were only friends we had no worries about you seeing each other. Recently. though it looks to both your father and me that you are becoming more than friends."

Jovinda looked her mother in the eyes. "And what if we are? He loves me, Mother, and I love him."

Ellire sighed as tears came into her eyes. "Darling, this cannot be. You are human and he's an elf."

Jovinda pressed her lips together and clenched her hands together. "Don't tell me you're objecting because he's different? He might be an elf and have a different background and upbringing, but we agree on so many things. We're friends as well as lovers. We laugh at the same things, get angry at the same things, enjoy the same things..."

Her mother held up her hand to stop her daughter. "Jo, Jo, I'm not against him personally. He's a very nice man, and so gallant and polite. If he were anything other than an elf I would not hesitate to agree to your relationship, but he *is* an elf."

"What difference does that make?"

"Quite a lot, actually. Elves live very long lives. I'm not quite sure how long, but some say nine hundred years. Humans live for seventy or eighty at the most. Darling, you will be an old, old woman while Noli is still young. Do you think he, a young man, will want to stay with an old woman?"

"He will. We've talked about this, Mother. He's promised he won't abandon me when I get old. He says he'll love me forever. Do you and Father not love one another even though you are both getting old?"

Ellire laughed. "Hardly old, dear. I'm only forty and your father forty-four. Anyway, we are both growing old together. That makes a big difference."

"Does it? What about Indro Manibrow? He left his wife for a younger woman only last year."

Ellire sighed again. "Your father and I are both in agreement that this must end before you get hurt, and get hurt you will if it goes on. We cannot allow it to get to the point where marriage is being considered. You must not see Noli again, Jovinda."

Jovinda burst into tears and fled to her room, threw herself onto her bed and sobbed.

* * *

Little did Jovinda know that Noli was having a similar conversation. He had come to Bluehaven in the company of his father. As a novice in diplomacy, he had much to learn. His father thought his son would learn a lot from seeing diplomats working at first hand.

"Son," Noli's father said, "I must ask you to desist from seeing this human girl."

Noli wrinkled his brow. "Why? Don't you like her?"

"Yes, I like her a lot, and if she were an elf, I wouldn't hesitate to encourage the relationship. She comes from a good family and is well brought up, but she's not an elf. She's a human and that makes all the difference."

"Father, surely you aren't one of those elves who think humans are inferior to us?"

"Of course not, boy. But humans are different. They have very short lives. How will you feel watching your love grow old and infirm while you are still young and healthy? How will you feel when she is sick and in pain and you watch her dying?"

"Father, I love her and I will to the end of my days. I will love her young or old, healthy or sick. I will not abandon her as she grows old."

"I'm sorry, my son, but I must forbid you from seeing her. I speak as both your father, and the leader of this mission."

Noli turned and stalked away, back to his rooms and stood at his window brooding and trying to think of a way out of this.

I will continue to see her. I love her. She's the best thing that has ever happened to me. But how can I see her? My father, as leader of the diplomatic mission, has forbidden me. He can fire me and send me back home if I disobey.

Noli continued to gaze out of the window.

I will go to see her. If my father sends me home, I will defy him again and stay here. I had better wait for a few days, though. Jo will understand when I tell her.

* * *

Jovinda stopped crying after several hours. She had no more tears. She lay on her bed looking out of the window at the clouds floating in a clear blue sky. The sun mocked her. She did not want to live. How could she, without Noli?

Rising, she walked towards the casement. She opened it and looked out, drawing a deep, sobbing breath. If she jumped from here she would only hurt herself. It was not high enough to kill her. She withdrew into the room.

A knock sounded on her door. She threw herself down on the bed and ignored it. The knock came again, followed by her mother's voice calling her name. Jovinda did not want to speak to her mother. She hated her, and her father, for forbidding her to see Noli.

Her mother called again, and then Jovinda heard a sigh and retreating footsteps. She rose again and went to the window where she sat on the window seat and gazed at the passers-by. There must be someway out of this. She must see Noli. What if he thought she did not want to see him? Would her parents allow her to go out alone? Probably not, knowing she would likely go to him.

After a long while and much thought, she had her plan sorted out. First she must go to see Salor. Her mother could accompany her if she wished. She was not going to go to try and see Noli. She must continue to act the broken-hearted girl though. If her parents thought she had recovered too quickly they would be suspicious. A few days would suffice.

For the next two days, Jovinda stayed impatiently in her room. She felt much happier now she had worked out her plan. Two days passed. She slowly opened the door and walked down the stairs into the hallway, keeping her eyes lowered and her mouth downcast. She was hungry. She had eaten very little during the last two days. She picked at the food her maid left outside her room wanting to appear to still be unhappy.

When she entered the dining-room, she sat at the table where her parents were beginning their meal.

Ellire smiled at her daughter. "Well, we're very glad to see you, Jo. We were worried about you up there on your own, weren't we, Kendo?"

"Yes, we were. You were hardly eating anything and not speaking to anyone. It's good to have you back at the table again." He turned to the butler. "Promin, serve Miss Jovinda with the soup, will you please?"

The meal passed with little conversation, and certainly nothing about Noli. Afterwards, Jovinda told her parents she was going to visit Salor that afternoon. She half expected an argument, but she was ready. After all, they could not legally stop a young woman of sixteen from going out.

Instead of an argument, Ellire said, "Oh, what a coincidence. I've planned to go to see Bremla this afternoon." She named Salor's mother. "I need to talk to her about the women's meeting next week. I'll walk with you."

Jovinda was not surprised her mother wanted to talk to Bremla. She knew it was a made-up excuse, but she pretended to be surprised and agreed. It would be pleasant to walk together.

* * *

Noli stood at his window for some time. He was not going to give this girl up. He loved her with all his heart and he believed she felt the same.

Later that day, he left the Rindissillaron Embassy where the elves were staying, and walked toward Jovinda's home. He had no idea what he was going to do. He stood in the street and looked up at the house. Where was she now? Was she in her room or had she gone out? Should he knock on the door? He had always been welcomed before. He decided he must see Jovinda and he crossed the street and raised the knocker on the door.

Promin answered. "I'm sorry, sir," he told Noli, "but Miss Jovinda is not entertaining today." He politely closed the door.

This happened for the next two days and Noli decided either Jovinda was no longer interested in him, which he did not believe, or her parents had a similar conversation with her as his father had with him. He must see her, but how?

He waited outside her house for two days and had not seen her. She must come out sometime. Her parents could not keep her inside against her will. She was, after all, an adult by the standards of the human world.

On the third day of waiting, Noli saw the front door open. His heart leaped as he saw his beloved coming down the steps, but it sank again when he saw that her mother accompanied her. He slipped down the street opposite and looked back to see Jovinda smile at something her mother said. She did not look unhappy. He sat down on the step of a nearby house. Perhaps it was true that she did not want to see him. His head sank into his hands and it was all he could do to prevent the tears.

He walked back to the embassy and entered. His father was about to leave to go to a meeting. "Where have you been? Hurry up and get ready. We have a meeting with the goldsmith's guild shortly. You need to come and learn about diplomacy and negotiating contracts. I hope you've not been seeing that girl."

"No, Father, I've not been seeing her. I'll be along in five minutes."

But I will see her again, and I will ask her if she wants to continue seeing me, have no fear of that.

* * *

Salor took Jovinda to her bedroom.

As soon as the door closed, Jovinda began to talk. "Salor, my parents have told me I'm not to see Noli again. Can you believe that?"

"Why? I thought they liked him."

"They do. At least, they say they do; but they are objecting because he's an elf."

Salor frowned. "They aren't prejudiced against elves, though—I know that—so why?"

"It's because elves live for hundreds of years, but humans live for less than one hundred. Even eighty is very old."

Salor nodded. "I can see it might be a problem. Even in humans, some people, usually men, leave their spouses when they're getting old and set up with a young person."

"Not you, too, Salor!"

"No. I'm not saying Noli will do that. I don't think he will, but I can see why your parents would object."

Jovinda stood and walked to the window, looking out at the people passing in the street below.

After a few seconds, she turned. "I'm an adult, Salor. I can do as I wish and they can't stop me. I want to see Noli. I will see Noli. I love him."

"This is so romantic."

"I want you to do me a favour. Have you got a pen and paper? I want to write a letter to Noli and I'm asking if you can somehow get it to him. I have a plan, but I need help to put it into action."

"Feel free to use the pen and paper on the desk in front of you."

Jovinda sat and wrote a brief note.

"How are we going to get it to him?" Salor asked.

"I've thought of that. Your maid can take it and give it to Noli's manservant. He's called Kifferissimos—or something that sounds like that."

The two girls plotted how the maid, Muren, could find out which of the elves was Kifferissimos and how she could get the note to him. It would not be easy, and Muren would need to be sworn to secrecy too.

They called the girl in and told her what they wanted her to do. She was as excited as Salor to be a go-between in an illicit affair. She suggested, if he were agreeable, that she and Kifferissimos could pretend to be lovers. That would be a good excuse to be seen together.

They agreed to the plan and Jovinda gave the note to Muren. Ellire called and Jovinda left Salor and ran down the stairs smiling at her mother.

"It's good to see you happy again." Ellire returned the smile. She turned to Bremla. "She's seeing the sense of what we told her about human and elf relationships. I'm so relieved."

The two girls exchanged guilty looks, unnoticed by either of the two older women.

* * *

Three anxious days passed. Jovinda could hardly contain herself. She could not rush around to see Salor every day, as that had not been their usual habit. There was sewing to be done and helping her mother with the household accounts. She took leftover food to some of the poor families. Those who did not live too far away, though, as it would not do for a well-bred young lady to venture into the poor district with all its dangers.

She visited the temple of Sylissa to help the clerics with the preparation of bandages. Each day she prayed at the temple of

Bramara, the goddess of the family and marriage, so that things would work out well for her and Noli.

Eventually, her patience paid off. Salor came to visit her one afternoon. When they were alone, Salor passed a note written in elegant handwriting. Jovinda could hardly contain herself. She held it to her breast for several minutes.

"Read it, Jo. You can write a reply and I can take it with me when I go."

Jovinda broke the seal.

My darling, Jo,

I hope you don't mind me calling you 'my darling', for you are indeed most dear to me. I read your note with excitement. Does this mean that you feel as strongly about me as I do about you? This I can hardly dare to hope for.

You tell me that your parents have forbidden you from seeing me. The same has happened here. My father is adamant that we do not see each other. I am sure they think that it is in our best interests, but I do not accept that.

Jo, my darling, I love you with all my heart. I cannot live without you. I WILL not live without you. It matters not one jot to me that you will grow old before me. I will love you exactly the same, young and old.

Please tell me how we can meet. I must see you again as soon as possible.

Yours forever,

Noli.

Tears filled Jovinda's eyes as she read the letter. Salor drew her brows together and reached out her hand to her friend.

"What does he say? You're crying. Is he finishing it?"

"No, Salor. I'm crying because it's such a beautiful letter. He says he loves me and how can we meet?"

The girls began to plot again. This time to work out how Jovinda and Noli could meet. They decided to plan a picnic.

Noli would 'accidentally' be walking past. Salor would remember she had to go somewhere, then the two lovers would be left alone.

* * *

The day of the picnic arrived. Salor came to Jovinda's home with a picnic basket and Jovinda picked up her own basket.

"Where are you going to have your picnic?" Ellire asked. "It's a beautiful day. The meadows down by the mouth of the Brundella would be nice."

"We thought we'd go up on the hill out of town," Jovinda replied. "There's a breeze up there and there are the woods if we need some shade. It might be a bit hot down by the river. There aren't many trees there."

They climbed the hill to the top and sat on the grass, spreading their picnic out in front of them. Jovinda arranged chicken legs and small meat pies on plates while Salor took salad leaves out of a bag and put them in a bowl. She picked up a box containing several small cakes and put them onto a plate and Jovinda poured cool drinks.

Jovinda was on tenterhooks and her hand shook, threatening to spill the drink she was pouring. *What if he doesn't come? What if he's changed his mind about me? What if his father's found out and has somehow prevented him from coming?*

Salor smiled, knowing what her friend was thinking. "He'll come, Jo. Don't you worry."

The girls began to eat, revelling in the sunshine and laughing at the antics of a squirrel that tried to pluck up enough courage to steal from their picnic.

Suddenly a figure strode out from the woods. The girls gave a little scream until Jovinda recognised her lover and leaped to her feet. She ran towards him, and he held out his arms to receive her.

Salor slipped away.

* * *

Jovinda went about her chores humming to herself. That afternoon she was going to see Noli again. It had been a week since she last saw him. It was not always easy for them to arrange their meetings. Noli had his work to do and they had to keep their meetings secret from their parents.

Salor helped the lovers. She thought it was exciting and romantic. She gave Jovinda alibis whenever the pair were to meet. If the girls met more than before, Jovinda's parents did not notice. At least, they made no comment. Perhaps they thought it was good for Jovinda to meet her friend rather than brood about Noli. But Jovinda did not care. She was seeing the man she loved.

Noli could not get away as often as he would have liked, but every time he had time to himself he and Jovinda would meet. Usually, they went to the woods out of town. It was quiet there and there were many places they could be alone with little fear of discovery.

* * *

The summer passed and the trees began to put on their autumn colours. Jovinda and Noli walked through a rain of falling leaves, their feet making swishing sounds as they passed through those lying on the ground.

"It sounds like walking through the waves on the sea," Jovinda said.

Finding themselves in an open glade, they sank to the

ground. "What are we going to do when winter's here" She turned to Noli, eyes full of worry. "It'll be cold and wet. We won't be able to sit on the ground then."

Noli looked at her and stroked her auburn hair. "Something will turn up, darling. We're meant to be together. I feel it deep inside my soul. Nothing will part us, not even winter."

He was right, of course.

As the last leaves fell from the trees and the summer warmth left the land, Jovinda came to a terrible realisation. She had missed her monthly bleeding. It was now time for the next one but still nothing happened. She had been in such ecstasy that she had not thought about anything other than Noli. Now she realised what the sickness she had felt when she rose in the mornings meant. She was pregnant.

How could she tell her parents? What would they do? Would they disown her? How would Noli react? Would he stand by her, or would he abandon her? Oh, why had she been so foolish? She had not thought about possible consequences when they had made love in their glade in the wood.

She had wanted to believe the tales that elves and humans could not create a child. She told herself that because she had never heard of a half-elf, half-human child, it must be true. Now she was suffering the results of that lack of forethought.

"I'm going to see Salor," she told her mother after she had finished her chores. Leaving the house she hurried to her friend's home. Salor had become engaged to a young man during the months that had passed and was due to be married in the spring. He was the son of a friend of her parents and both sets of parents were delighted with the engagement.

It was so different from Jovinda and Noli's experience that Jovinda was a little jealous. Yet, she would not change Noli in any way, even for approval by her parents.

She arrived at Salor's house, and their butler admitted her.

Salor led her to her bedroom. Once inside, Jovinda burst into tears.

"What's wrong, Jovinda? It's not a problem with Noli, is it?"

Jovinda dried her eyes and sighed. "Well, it is and it isn't. Oh, Salor, I'm in so much trouble. I've missed two monthly bleedings."

Salor put her hand to her mouth. "That means…"

"Yes. I'm pregnant."

Salor looked at her friend with eyes open wide. "I didn't think you'd be so foolish, Jo. How did you not think this might happen?"

Jovinda's eyes began to leak tears again as she tried to push them back. "I didn't think. Well, I thought with him being an elf it couldn't happen. Oh, Salor, it felt so right. We love one another and soon kisses weren't enough to show our love. What am I to do?"

"Does he know?"

Jovinda shook her head. "I've not seen him since I realised."

"Will he marry you? Or do you want to go to a witch woman and get rid of it?"

"I don't know." Jovinda wailed and started crying again.

"Well, you must tell Noli, Jo. He's as much to blame as you. Why do the girls always have to take the worst of the blame for things like this?"

Jovinda sobbed and Salor rooted in a draw for a handkerchief for her. Handing it to her friend, she said "I hope Noli isn't one of those men who run away from responsibility. I've seen young women left with an unwanted baby when the father decided he didn't want a wife and child."

Jovinda blew her nose and took a breath, but Salor continued.

"They have their fun, and then run when the consequences

become clear, leaving the poor girl, her reputation in tatters, to deal with it all."

Jo looked at her friend with eyes red with tears. "Noli isn't like that, Salor"

"No? I hope you're right, Jo, and that he'll marry you. It's different if the man marries the girl. Oh, there's always a scandal at first, but later people conveniently forget the child's rather early birth or when the wedding was."

Salor told Jovinda she would help her get a message to Noli, asking to meet at their usual place the following day.

* * *

It was cold. The fallen leaves made a multicoloured carpet on the ground in the clearing in the woods where Noli waited. He pulled his cloak around himself as he wondered what Jovinda wanted to see him about so urgently. Her note had said it was essential she see him as soon as possible.

He had needed to make an excuse to his father to be able to leave his work early. He heard a crackle in the leaves and turned to see Jovinda crossing the glade. He opened his arms and she ran into them. They kissed passionately before saying a word.

He looked into his lover's eyes and saw they were red. She had been crying. Had her parents found out about them? He held her close and waited for her to speak.

"Noli," she said through her tears, "I'm pregnant. I'm thinking of going to a witch woman to get rid of it though."

For the first time since they met, Noli became angry. He pressed his lips together then thrust her away.

"You will not kill this child." He stalked to the opposite side of the glade and turned, his indigo eyes looking like stormy skies. "It's a new life beginning. Who knows what great deeds it could do, or how important its descendants could be. We elves will never destroy a life, even an unborn one."

"But, Noli, what are we to do?"

He came back to her side, anger forgotten. He could not stay angry at his love. He put his arms around her again. "We'll get married, sweetheart. It's what I would like, and I hope you would like it, too."

Jovinda beamed. "Of course I would like that. We can have this baby and then lots more."

Noli laughed. "I hope so. Elves aren't very fertile as a rule. I suppose it's because we live so long. If we had too many children, we'd soon overrun the world. But an elf and a human... who knows?"

He held her close and whispered in her ear. "Darling, your parents will be so angry. What will they do?"

Jovinda shuddered and clung closer to him. "I don't know." Tears sprang from her eyes, and she hid them in his shoulder. "I hope they won't disown me."

Noli frowned and held her at arms length. "They wouldn't do that, would they?"

She turned away. "I don't know. It's such a disgrace, having a child before marriage. I really don't know what they'll do. I couldn't bear it if they disowned me." She looked into his eyes. "I love them, Noli, in spite of them trying to separate us. I would hate never to see them again."

"I don't think that will happen, though, Jo. They love you, too. They'll be shocked and angry, yes, but they'll come round. I'll come with you when you tell them. I'll give you support and tell them I won't abandon you."

Jovinda shook her head. "No. Your presence would make things worse. It's better if I tell them alone."

They parted, he to tell his father and she to tell her parents. Neither looked forward to those interviews

* * *

Jovinda dragged her feet as she walked back home. She resolved to confess to her parents the very next day.

The following morning, Jovinda got up with a feeling of dread in her stomach that was more than morning sickness. How was she going to tell her parents about her pregnancy and how would they react?

She put it off until after the mid-day meal. When they retired to the sitting room, she screwed up her courage. "Mother, Father, I have something to tell you." She paused and took a deep breath.

"What is it, Jo?" Kendo asked.

The girl's eyes filled with tears. "There's no easy way to say this," she said as the tears fell. "I'm pregnant."

Her mother gave a gasp, then surged to her feet and slapped her daughter across the face. "You little slut. Who's the father? If you even know!"

It was Jovinda's turn to gasp. The tears that had started to fall at her mother's reaction dried up. Her fear and sorrow turned into anger at the implication held in those words.

"Are you suggesting I've slept with lots of men? I would never sleep with anyone if I were not in love with him. There's only one man in my life, and that's Noli. He's the father of my child."

"That's immaterial," her mother retorted. "One man or ten, you've brought disgrace to our family. Your father was likely to get re-elected to the leadership the guilds in the next few months. A scandal like this could lose that for him. And what about our friends and neighbours? What will they think?"

Kendo gently took hold of Ellire's hand as she raised it to slap her daughter again. "Let's talk about this calmly." He led his wife back to the chair she had occupied. He looked at her with gentle eyes. "Ell, my dear, our daughter's mistake is unlikely to have any impact on my election to the guild leadership. There are things that can be done about this."

Jovinda looked at her father. She still felt angry at her mother's reaction and did not like what his words implied.

"Are you suggesting going to a witch and getting rid of the child? This is a new life growing in me. I refuse to kill it."

Ellire calmed down at her husband's words. "Jovinda, that's the perfect solution. No one need know. Have you told anyone yet?"

"I've told Noli and Salor. And it isn't the perfect solution. This child has two parents. Me and Noli. He has a right to have a say in what happens to it, as he would if it had been born in wedlock. He says elves revere life and will not take it unnecessarily. Abortion would be unnecessary in this case. Anyway, he wants to marry me."

On hearing this, Ellire began to cry. Kendo took her arm and led her to the door. "You go and lie down, Ell. Let me deal with this."

He came back to talk to Jovinda and sat in the chair opposite her. "Darling, please don't take any notice of what your mother says. This had been a big shock to her, as it has to me. I didn't think it of you. Still, it's happened, and we must decide, calmly, I might add, what the next step should be."

Jovinda looked into her father's eyes. "The next step is that Noli and I will get married. I would not have had it happen like this, but it has. I don't regret what Noli and I did. I don't think I regret being pregnant except for what you and mother think. Noli and I will get married whatever you say. I don't need your permission. I'm over sixteen. I would like your blessing, but with or without it, I will marry him."

Kendo sighed. "I see we have no choice. There'll be a scandal for a while, but people will forget. There'll be something else for them to talk about that will take its place. I wish this hadn't happened, but it has. I'll go and talk to your mother now and see what I can do. You'd better keep out of her way for a bit." He smiled at his daughter as he left the room

* * *

When Ellire spoke to Noli's father she found he was no more pleased than she, but all three parents came to accept that the marriage would, no must, as Ellire said, take place as soon as possible. The baby would be due in the spring.

"But Mother," Jovinda said, "I would like to get married on the feast of Bramara. It's good luck to all couples who get married on that day."

Ellire shook her head. On this she was adamant. She had given in to Jovinda's insistence that the couple get married, and she would have the baby, but she would not countenance waiting until the winter solstice.

"After all, it won't be possible to pass off the birth as premature if we wait so long. And your condition will be obvious by then."

It was not the wedding Ellire had foreseen for her daughter. She had imagined a large wedding with lots of guests, her daughter looking radiant and beautiful, with her husband a shadowy figure in the background. She would have been the perfect hostess dressed in beautiful clothes bought for the occasion.

Now, instead, was this shady marriage. Oh, it was in the temple of Bramara, but there were few guests. Salor attended Jovinda and a young elf she had not seen before attended Noli. Salor's parents were present as well as Noli's father and another couple of elves. The only thing she had foreseen was Jovinda's radiant expression. Her daughter did look beautiful, she had to admit, with her hair flowing down her back, brushed to a gleaming copper. Her eyes shone, as did Noli's deep blue ones. There was no doubt they loved each other.

After the ceremony they all went back to the house she shared with Kendo for the wedding feast.

The meal was a special one, as expected at a wedding, but not as lavish as Ellire would have liked for the marriage of her only child.

The guests gathered in the drawing room and drank glasses of Perimo. A maid walked around with a tray of small savouries for the guests.

Ellire looked around. There were not many guests for the wedding of the daughter of the Leader of the Guilds. She gave a slight shake of her head and took a sip of her wine. She spoke to each of the people gathered in the room with a fixed smile on her face.

Promin entered and announced that the meal was ready. Ellire took the arm of Noli's father and led the party into the dining room. On entering, she looked around to ensure everything was as she had planned it. This might be a rushed wedding, but Ellire wanted everything to be as perfect as possible. After all, she had her reputation as a hostess to consider.

The table had been covered with a white cloth. Silver cutlery graced each place with a silver mat. More silver mats sat along the length of the table, and a bowl of late blooming white flowers graced the centre. At each place were cut-glass wine and water glasses.

Ellire nodded her approval at Promin, who gave a slight bow of acknowledgement.

Everyone waited behind their chairs until the bride and groom entered. The newlyweds sat at the head of the table, both looking radiant.

The meal began with a puff pastry case filled with crab and prawns. It was served with glasses of a dry white wine.

Promin carved a leg of lamb for the second course and served it first to Jovinda and Noli, and then to the rest of the guests. Bowls of vegetables and rice stood on the table ready for the guests to serve themselves. He then filled the guests' glasses with a fine red wine.

After the guests finished the meat course, Promin gave each one a small wooden platter with five different cheeses, all from the local area, and biscuits to eat with them.

When he had cleared all this away, Promin disappeared and then reappeared with the dessert. Everyone gasped as he entered carrying a confection composed of meringue filled with strawberries. It looked like an enormous nest, with little chocolate birds perched on the side, and some on thin wires 'flying' above it.

"It's far too beautiful to eat," Jovinda whispered to Noli.

He smiled at his new wife. "But I don't suppose you'll refuse some."

She giggled. "No, of course not. I love chocolate and strawberries."

The party soon made short work of the dessert, even though some thought, like Jovinda, that it was too beautiful to cut into. They drank the sweet white wine Promin served with it and declared it to be a perfect complement to the sweetness of the dessert.

After that had been cleared away, and small cups of coffee drunk, Kendo stood up and tapped his spoon on a glass.

"I would like to say a word, please. We all know of Jo's pregnancy, and I must say we were none too pleased when she told us, but we have come to terms with that now." He stared at Ellire as if challenging her to argue. She looked down at her hands clasped in her lap. "We are now looking forward to welcoming our grandchild in the spring. So, to show we are now happy with our new son-in-law, we have bought a house for them."

Jovinda stared at her father open-mouthed and Noli's eyes nearly popped out of his head.

Kendo continued. "The house is not as large as this one, but it's big enough for three and has a garden. What's more, it's not too far from here so when our grandson or daughter arrives, we can see lots of him or her. Here are the keys, Jovinda and Noli. I hope you like it."

Before he could sit down, Jovinda jumped up and threw her arms around her father. "Oh, Thank you, thank you, Father. I know you didn't mind us staying here, but to have our own place..." She broke down crying as Noli hugged her and said his thanks to his father-in-law.

As Ellire turned her head to look at them, a smile crept onto her face. She had agreed to the purchase of the house, but had not yet come to terms with the fact that her daughter had become pregnant out of wedlock, but seeing the joy on her Jovinda's face, she could not help but feel happy for her.

Then her smile faded as Kendo looked at her. He's trying to make me happy with this relationship, but I know it will end in tears.

* * *

Jovinda and Noli moved into the house Kendo had given them two weeks later. Noli's father was generous enough to pay for some of the furniture, and although the house was not filled, they had enough.

The house was two streets away from Jovinda's old home. It was a three storey house with a small garden and four bedrooms.

In the small cul-de-sac there were half a dozen houses in a terrace on each side of the road

Jovinda and Noli stood outside, hand in hand, and staring at the house. "I can't believe this is ours." Jovinda said.

"Your father was most generous, darling. It's perfect."

They walked up the path to the front door and Jovinda turned the key. The door swung open and they entered.

Jovinda scanned the hallway. It ran the length of the house with stairs mounting up the left hand side. A door opened to their right and they entered a living room with a bay window.

"It'll get lots of sunshine in here," Noli pointed out. "Let's go and look at the other rooms."

The next door in the hallway opened into a room a little smaller than the front one. Jovinda went to Look out of the window,

"Oh, this room looks over the garden, Noli. Come and look. It's lovely." She turned away from the window and her eyes glanced around the room. "This will be our dining room."

Continuing down the hallway they found it turned right to a door, and another door stood before them. This one led to a kitchen with a range on the left hand wall and windows opposite.

"We need a table in here for preparing food," Jovinda said as she opened another door opposite where they had entered. "Oh! This is a pantry."

On opening the final door at the end of the hallway, they found themselves in the garden. It had a lawn, a few fruit trees and lots of flowerbeds.

"I'll love sitting here in the summer, Noli. And I can plant lots of flowers. It's perfect."

"Come on, Jo. We need to look upstairs."

Climbing the stairs, Jovinda found two bedrooms. The final flight of stairs led to two further small rooms in the attic.

Ellire had said they should have a cook at the very least, and a maid, as Jovinda would be unable to do all the cleaning in the coming months, as she became bigger with the child. She found a woman whom her own cook recommended and a young girl with some experience as a maid. As both lived not too far away, they did not need to live in.

"I've no idea about what sort of person is best for these jobs," she told Noli. "I'm so glad Mother has done it for me."

Jovinda declared she must have a nurse for the coming baby as befitted her station as the wife of a diplomat and daughter of the Leader of the Guilds and Noli indulged her. They spent many hours setting up the nursery and nurse's room on the top floor of the house.

Three weeks before the baby was due, Noli and Jovinda interviewed several candidates for the job of nurse and appointed a woman in her early forties. Her name was Blendin and she came with excellent references. They decided she should move in right away so she would be settled by the time the baby arrived.

The late-spring had been hot. Much hotter than usual. The baby was due on the twenty fifth day of Zoldar, the last month of spring. That day came and went, then five more. Jovinda waddled into their living room wiping the sweat from her brow and flopped down into a chair.

She rang a bell and the maid arrived. "Please, may I have some water?"

The maid left to do her mistress's bidding.

Jovinda and Noli were not amongst the richest of Blue-haven, he being a junior diplomat, but they were well enough off to be able to afford their maid and cook. Jovinda was most grateful for the help these servants gave her as her confinement approached. How she would be glad when this baby arrived. It was so uncomfortable in the hot weather.

The maid returned with a jug of water and a glass. She poured some into the glass and handed it to Jovinda. Suddenly, a pain struck. Jovinda gasped.

"Please, Grella, go and get Blendin, then run to the Elven Embassy and find Noli. I think the baby's coming."

The girl shot out of the room, and Blendin arrived almost immediately afterwards.

Jovinda had no more pains and she wondered if it had been indigestion and not the baby, but then she was wracked with another.

"It's the baby coming, all right," Blendin said, putting her hand on Jovinda's abdomen as the pain struck and nodding her head. "Your muscles are tightening when you get the pain. The pains aren't too close together yet, so there'll be some time before we need to send for the midwife. Let's get you upstairs and have things ready for when she comes."

In this instance she was wrong. Shortly after arriving in the bedroom, Jovinda's waters broke. Then the pains came thick and fast. No sooner had one pain faded away than another arrived. Jovinda began to cry.

"Make it stop. Please, Bramara, make it stop." Jovinda prayed to the goddess of marriage and the family.

Blendin wiped the girl's sweating brow with a cloth dipped in cool water. "There, there. The only way it'll stop is when the baby arrives. It shouldn't be too long now."

"To the seventh hell with the baby," Jovinda retorted. "The little bastard is tearing me apart."

She began to swear profusely and to say she cared nothing for the child struggling to be born. If her father and mother had heard those words coming from their well-brought-up daughter they would have wondered where she learned them.

"I don't care if there's no baby, but please make this pain stop." Then she felt her muscles contract involuntarily and she began to push. So strong was the instinct that if a warrior with an axe stood there and demanded she did not do so, she could not have complied.

"Come on." Blendin encouraged her. "Push hard. Oh, I can see the baby's head."

Jovinda gave one last enormous push and the head emerged followed by the rest of the baby, all wet and bloody.

Blendin held the child up so Jovinda could see. "A little boy, and he's got your auburn hair."

The baby let out a tremendous wail at being thrust from his warm, safe place into the cold world. "And a good strong pair of lungs, too," Blendin added with a laugh.

At that moment, the door opened and Noli and the midwife arrived together.

Noli rushed over to his wife and looked at Blendin. "Is everything all right? It must have happened very quickly. Is Jo all right? Is the baby all right?"

Jovinda laughed through the tiredness that now overcame her. "Yes, everything is fine now, Noli."

The midwife took over. She tied a piece of leather around the cord before cutting it then handed the crying baby to Jovinda, who grinned to see him. Another pain came as the baby turned toward Jovinda's breast.

"Let him suckle," the midwife told her. "It'll help drive the afterbirth out."

Jovinda did as the midwife told her and she felt the contractions as the baby fed. Soon the midwife exclaimed the afterbirth had come away and she began her inspection of it.

Blendin took the baby and cleaned him. He began to cry again at being taken from his meal, but once washed and dressed in the clothes laid out for him he settled down.

When the midwife finished her inspection, she declared

everything to be all right and she turned to Noli. "Your wife, had an easy birth, so Blendin tells me."

Jovinda grimaced. Easy? It felt like hard work. And painful work, too.

The midwife continued. "It's lucky your nurse has some experience in delivering babies, but I think your wife would have been fine even on her own. It's women like her who ought to have all the babies."

Jovinda yawned, then said "Oh no. You say it was easy, but to me it wasn't. It was the hardest thing I've ever done."

"Trust me, girl," the midwife replied. "There are women who are in labour for days, and then the baby has to be pulled out, or even cut out."

Jovinda shuddered. As Blendin passed the little boy to her, she held him out to his father. "See, Noli. See what we've made. A lovely little boy. What shall we call him?"

"Carthinal's a good name, what do you think?"

"Carthinal." She felt the name on her tongue. "Yes, an excellent name." She looked into the little boy's eyes, deep blue like those of his father. All pain forgotten, she said, with a smile, "Welcome to the world, Carthinal."

Two years passed, and Carthinal was toddling about. Noli came in from the embassy where he was still working. It was Carthinal's second birthday and he had brought a huge toy dog for his son.

"Dada," Carthinal said. He ran toward his father.

Noli gave him the dog and Carthinal struggled with it, dragging the toy toward the sitting room where he had been spending some time with Jovinda. She laughed at his difficulty, then went to help him bring it in.

"Say thank you to Daddy, Carthinal," Jovinda said.

"Fan choo," Carthinal looked at his father. "Fan choo. Doggy."

Jovinda kissed her husband. "I'm a bit worried about Carthinal, Noli. Most of my friends' children his age are much more advanced. Even some of those much younger are further along than he is. I'm afraid there's something wrong. Perhaps he's not very bright."

Noli laughed. "There's nothing wrong with our son, Jo. Half his blood is elf. Elven children develop more slowly than human ones. In fact, he's in advance of most elven children of his age." He paused for a minute. "I don't know how quickly or slowly this mixture of elf and human will develop, but probably about half way between an elf child and a human one, I would say. It'll be interesting to find out. In the meantime, stop worrying."

Jovinda smiled at her husband and picked up her son, dog and all. She kissed him as he tried to get down again.

"Down," he insisted. He clenched his small fist and tried to punch her. "Down," he repeated.

Noli took his hand. "You must not punch your mother, Carthinal. That's very naughty."

"Want down," he said. His deep blue eyes, so much like his father's, grew even deeper.

Jovinda put him down and sighed. "That's another thing. He's developing a temper. We must nip that in the bud."

"No one said bringing up a child is easy, love. In fact, it's the hardest thing in the world. You're doing a great job."

The couple wished for another child, but the years passed and there was no sign. Noli said it was due to the infertility of elves and that it would happen in due course. Jovinda went to the temple of Bramara and prayed, but to no avail.

When Carthinal was six, he was playing on a swing Kendo had fixed to the branch of a tree in the garden. He heard his nurse calling for him, but took no notice. It was nice in the garden. The sun was shining and he liked the swing.

Shortly, Jovinda came out and saw him. "Oh, there you are. Didn't you hear nurse calling for you?"

"Yes, but I don't want to go in. I like it out here."

"You must come in now, Carthinal. It's time for your tea and then it's bathtime and bedtime."

The little boy's face clouded over and he fixed his lips into a straight line. "Shan't."

"Oh, don't be naughty, Carthinal. Be a good boy and come for your tea."

"No." His eyes changed from blue summer skies to dark stormy seas. Jovinda noticed the change. She went and picked him off the swing, carrying him, squirming and crying into the house. She handed him over to Blendin who took him away for his tea.

Jovinda went into the sitting room and smiled. She had become used to these infrequent outbursts of temper and knew that in a few minutes her son would be his normal sunny self again. His temper tantrums never lasted long. He would soon come downstairs and apologise, then wait for cuddles.

Noli arrived soon after this and sank down in one of the chairs. "There's a problem in Rindisillaron. The Elflord has died and there's an argument about the succession."

"I thought the Elflord was succeeded by the eldest male child of his nearest female relative."

"Yes, That's true, but in this case there are identical twins."

"So! The elder twin inherits, doesn't he?"

"Ah, therein lies the problem. You see, when the twins were born, their mother was ill after the birth and in the rush to treat her the twins weren't labelled. Now both twins are claiming to be the first-born."

Noli crossed his legs and leaned back.

"The father told the midwife the first child was to be called Frissillimidor and the second Grimmshollin. The midwife claimed she knew in which crib she'd put each baby and so they were named."

He stood and walked around the room before continuing.

"I believe the midwife would have been correct and that Frissillimidor is the elder, but factions have grown up, as you would expect. Now war has broken out."

"That doesn't affect us herein Bluehaven, though." Jovinda frowned. "We aren't involved in Elven politics."

Noli came and sat on the arm of the chair his wife sat in and took her hand. "You aren't involved. Bluehaven isn't involved, but I'm an elf, and so I am involved, like it or not. Father is packing at this minute to go to help the rightful heir."

Jovinda turned and looked at her husband, understanding beginning to dawn on her face. "So you plan to go and fight too."

Noli nodded, his eyes sad. He looked at his feet.

"You'd leave your wife and child for this war?" Jovinda's eyes narrowed and her lips pressed together. Anger rather than sadness at the thought of Noli going away swept through her. She stood, hands on hips and stared at Noli. "You care more for this Frissi-whatsit than Carthinal and me?"

Noli stood. "Not at all, Jo. You know I love you and Carthinal more than life itself." He went over and tried to put his arm around her, but she shrugged it off. "Darling, it's not a matter of what I want, but of duty. I cannot let the wrong person take the throne."

Jovinda stepped away from him, eyes hard.

"Jo, Jo, please understand. Imagine it was here in Grosmer and the wrong man was about to ascend the throne. You wouldn't want Carthinal, if he were of age, to stand by and allow it to happen, would you?"

No matter what argument she put forward, Noli was

adamant he must go to fight for the rightful heir. The couple went to bed that evening in silence that continued until three days later.

The day before Noli was due to leave, Jovinda stood in front of him.

She put her arms around him and leaned her head against his shoulder. "I can't let you go without saying I'm sorry."

He took her in his arms and kissed her. "You've nothing to be sorry for. You have every right to be angry, but this is my land —my people—whose future is in the balance. I have to go, even though I'd much rather stay here with you and Carthinal."

Jovinda said goodbye to Noli with a heavy heart. She stood on the doorstep of their house with Carthinal as she saw him off. She blinked back her tears as she stood waving until he could no longer be seen.

"How long will Daddy be away?" Carthinal asked.

"I don't know, dear. He'll come and see us when he gets leave."

* * *

Two years passed. Noli came home as often as he could, but he needed a long leave to make the journey to Bluehaven from Rindissillaron and back and he had little time left when he was there. Jovinda had to rely on his letters to tell her of the progress of the war.

In one letter, Noli wrote of how the war was nearly won. Grimmshollin had retreated to a very small area and was barely holding it. It would be only a few days before the war was over.

Jovinda grinned at receiving this news and looked forward to welcoming Noli home. Every day she expected a letter, or even Noli himself to arrive. The letter came in a sixday saying there was one more battle to end the war and then a few things to sort out before he could come home. She was ecstatic and began to prepare a welcome party.

A couple of sixdays later, there was a knock on the door. The maid answered and showed an officer into the drawing room where Jovinda sat reading to Carthinal. She rose as the officer entered.

He saluted and introduced himself as Roshinderal, Noli's friend.

"Yes, he's spoken of you often in his letters," Jovinda said. "Do you know when he'll be home? I'm planning a welcome home party for him, you see."

The young captain cleared his throat and shuffled his feet, looking at the floor. "You'd better send your son out of the room, Madam."

Jovinda's heart began to race as she told Carthinal to go to the nursery. At first she though he would refuse. She saw the tell-tale signs come over his face, but the boy thought better of it and left.

"Please, sit down," Roshinderal said, as though it were his house and she were the visitor.

Jovinda sat on her chair as requested, heart sinking.

Roshinderal cleared his throat again and began to speak. "It was the last battle, and nearly the end of that too. The enemy was retreating. Noli laughed and said he always knew we'd win as we were in the right. At that moment, one of the enemy archers turned and drew his bow. The arrow took Noli."

Jovinda's hand went to her mouth. "How is he? Can I go to see him? Is he badly injured?"

Roshinderal took Jovinda's hand in his. "I'm sorry to be the bearer of this news, but I'm afraid Noli died of his injuries soon afterwards. The arrow ruptured an artery. He knew he was dying and asked me to come and tell you that he loves you more than he could ever express. He said to take care of Carthinal. He was very proud of you both."

Jovinda looked at Roshinderal with a blank look in her eyes. All the life had gone out of them. Then she screamed. "No! No! No! It's not true. You've all made a mistake. He's not dead. He can't be. Go back and check. I'd know if he was dead. I know I would. I'd feel it in my heart." She shook her head vigorously in disbelief, refusing to accept what Roshinderal had told her.

Putting her fingers in her hair, she grabbed handfuls. She pulled hard, as if the physical pain would stop the pain in her heart.

Her screams brought the maid, who was passing the door. "Madam. What's the matter? Is it this man? Do you want him to leave?"

Roshinderal turned to the girl. "I've brought her bad news. Her husband was killed in the last battle of the war. Is there anyone whom I can get to be with her?"

Between them, they decided Jovinda's parents would be the best people to look after her and so Roshinderal set off to their house to get them.

As soon as they arrived, they took Jovinda and Carthinal, along with Blendin, his nanny, back to their house. Ellire took Jovinda and put her to bed in her old room with a soothing drink and soon she fell asleep.

Jovinda remained in her room for the next few days. She refused to answer the door, so Ellire left a tray outside. Some days a little of it disappeared, but on others Jovinda did not touch it.

Ellire tried talking to her daughter through the door, but got no response. She tried to get her to come out to see Carthinal who wondered what was going on. The eight-year-old under-stood his father had been killed in the war and had been incon-solable for a few days, but then, in the way of children, he bounced back somewhat. He could not, however, understand why his mother ignored him. He sat on the ground outside her room and talked to her through the door.

"Mummy, please come out. I miss you. I want to give you a big cuddle." Tears began to form in the child's eyes, but he blinked them back. "I know you miss Daddy. I miss Daddy, too, but I know he can't come back. Please let me give you the big hug I know Daddy would want me to."

Ellire tried to tell Jovinda how much her son missed her. Either the young woman did not hear or she was still too much enveloped in grief that she did not care.

Three days passed and Jovinda had not responded to anything. The trays of food and drink had been left untouched and no sounds came from her room. No sobs, no crying, no prayers, nothing.

Kendo decided he would go in. After all, no one could go without food and drink indefinitely, and Jovinda had not drunk or eaten anything in three days. He knocked on the door. No sound from inside. He tried the latch, but the door was locked.

Frowning, he called again, and when he still received no answer he said, "Jo, if you don't answer me I'm going to break the door."

Still nothing. Kendo put his shoulder to the door and pushed. The door did not move. He listened again. Still no sound from inside the room. He stepped back and ran at the door, hitting it with his shoulder. It moved, but did not give way. He rubbed his shoulder and ran at it again. This time there was a cracking noise as the hinges gave way and he fell into the room.

What he saw there broke his heart. There was his daughter, swinging from the beams overhead, a belt around her neck. He quickly cut her down, but it was to no avail. She had been dead for quite some time. A couple of days, probably.

He left the room and told Ellire not to go in and to keep Carthinal away.

Kendo went out into the garden and sat under a tree. Was there something he should have done? He ought to have broken the door down sooner. They should have insisted Jovinda come out and eat her meals with them. She had been brooding in there alone. All these thoughts went through his head until he felt he was going to go mad.

* * *

They held the funeral in the temple of Kalhera a few days later. The family was surprised at how many people turned up. Jovinda and Noli were popular figures in Bluehaven. Kendo knew he would never get over his guilt about his daughter's death, but he buried it deep.

He spoke to his wife after the funeral, when everyone had left and Ellire was weeping softly.

"There's Carthinal to consider, Ellire. He'll need a lot of support and help. We need to be his anchor now that Jo's gone."

Ellire blew her nose. "Yes, of course. We'll need to bring him up. We should sell Jo and Noli's house and put the money in trust for him. He'll live here now with us."

"Should we tell him how his mother died, do you think?"

"No. At least not for a long while. The poor child's had enough to cope with without knowing his mother killed herself."

Thus Carthinal lived with his grandparents and they brought him up. No one ever told him how his mother died.

The End

The story continues in:
The Wolf Pack by V.M. Sang

To read the first chapter for free, please head to:
https://www.nextchapter.pub/books/the-wolf-pack

Thank you for reading this story.

If you want to find out more about Carthinal, you can buy The Wolves of Vimar Series from Amazon.

Book 1: The Wolf Pack

http://mybook.to/TheWolfPack

Book 2: The Never-Dying Man

http://mybook.to/TheNeverDyingMan

Bookl 3: Wolf Moon

http://mybook.to/WolfMoonVM

I would be most grateful for a review of this novella. Writers rely on reviews to bring their work to the notice of the wider reading public.

If you have posted a review, Thank you.

ACKNOWLEDGMENTS

I would like to thank Miika Hannila and all the staff at Next Chapter, who work so hard to get our books out so you can read and enjoy them.

ABOUT THE AUTHOR

V.M. Sang was born and lived her early life in Cheshire in the north west of England

She has always loved books and reading and learned to read before she went to school.

A book by Enid Blyton, called Shadow the Sheepdog that V.M. Sang loved, with her love of animals. inspired her to write her very first story, the tale of a dog.

During her teenage years she wrote some poetry, one of which was published in the magazine of the University of Manchester Institute of Science and Technology (UMIST).

V.M. Sang became a teacher and taught English Science and Maths Her main subject was science, though, but she also taught what was then known as Computer Studies.

A 9 year old boy told her she should read The Lord of the Rings, but first read The Hobbit. This she did and have been hooked on fantasy ever since.

She did little writing until starting to teach in Croydon, Greater London. Here she started a Dungeons and Dragons club in the school using bought scenariosbefore beginning to write her own.

The idea of turning it into a novel formed in her head and she began to write The Wolves of Vimar Series

Walking has always been one of V.M. Sang's favourite pastimes, having gone on walking holidays in her teens. She met her husband walking with the University Hiking Club, and they still enjoy walking on the South Downs.

She enjoys a variety of crafts, such as card making, tatting, crochet, knitting etc. she also draws and paints.

V.M.Sang is married with two children, a daughter and a son. Her daughter has three children and she loves to spend time with them.

She now lives in East Sussex with her husband.

V.M. Sang author page at Next Chapter:
https://www.nextchapter.pub/authors/vm-sang

Lightning Source UK Ltd.
Milton Keynes UK
UKHW022340190121
377353UK00010B/667/J